Contents

Special Mentions

Behind the Scenes

Gilesgate Story Challenge 2020

Once upon a time...

...in Gilesgate, a spark of an idea came to life.

Books are fun. A good story always stirs something inside of us. Children of all abilities are capable of the most fantastic creations when given time and freedom to imagine.

In a world of SATs, league tables and electronic distractions maybe people on all sides need reminding that story-telling is fun, and important.

This idea starts, as so many stories start, with a thought:

"I wonder if...

Welcome to the Gilesgate Story Challenge, Volume 2.

Foreword

By Simon Berry

Welcome to a new year and a new competition. And what a strange year this has been!

In 2019 we launched the first ever Gilesgate Story Challenge. We asked for stories that were all about eyes and vision. Everyone involved was a little surprised and saddened that almost half of the stories we received talked about being bullied when wearing a pair of glasses.

That surprise added to a feeling that the world at the beginning of 2020 was becoming a gloomy place. People were being cruel on social media. The mainstream media was full of criticism and judgement. We seemed to be losing our spark of light.

All of this inspired the subject of this years competition. I wanted a bit of good news and something to refresh us from all the bullying and cruelty. So we asked our authors for stories of Random Acts of Kindness.

We launched the Gilesgate Story Challenge 2 with a splash of local publicity and eight of our local schools supporting us. Little did we know what was about to happen.

A horrible illness started spreading around the world. A virus that was about to change everything for everyone.

With no vaccine and no cure, the only way to stop the spread of the disease was for everyone to leave school and work, to stop seeing friends and to stay at home. We were very quickly all in a lockdown to try and save lives.

The world became an incredibly dark, scary place. Our lives were turned upside-down within the space of a few days. Suddenly, the subject of our short story competition became so much more apt. The world seemed to need random acts of kindness more than it ever did.

But then, did it?

An amazing thing started spreading around every corner of humanity. Faster than the virus ever could. Every where we looked people were being kind and trying to help each other.

Randomly, people in Spain and Italy started cheering the doctors and nurses that were looking after their loved ones. The idea quickly spread to the UK and became a weekly celebration of our selfless healthcare staff.

People started drawing rainbows in windows and painting stones to cheer people up and brighten their day.

People reacted when they were needed. When there was a shortage of face masks, they started printing them and making them at home. When there was a shortage of ventilators, manufacturers changed production lines to make sure we didn't run out. When frontline workers ended up missing lunch because they were too busy, people set up ways to bring them food.

People wanted to help. The NHS put out a call for volunteers and within 2 days had over 750,000 applicants. Their website couldn't cope and had to shut down applications. A 99 year old man with a modest aim of raising £1000 ended up raising £32 million and inspiring a nation.

Communities supported each other. People set up groups for neighbours, they checked in on vulnerable people. They delivered groceries. They made sure they everyone had some sort of human contact.

Every single person reading this did what they could to help someone else, and that made a huge difference.

This is not random.

Acts of kindness are never random because they are an integral part of our human make-up. We exist to be nice to people.

But we are also influenced by the crowd and what other people are doing. Being nice and kind doesn't often make the headlines or create as many 'likes' or 'shares.' Good news doesn't sell as many newspapers as gossip. When all we hear about is cruelty and criticism then we risk to lose a little bit of our humanity.

We need a big shove in the right direction. And a great way to start is to read the stories in this book and start to create our own Super Secret Society of Kindness.

If everyone is being cruel on social media - so what? Post something nice.

If all you you hear is people criticising others - so what? Encourage and congratulate.

Let us stop buying into this myth that everyone is out there for themselves. The amazing stories that you are about to read should serve as a reminder of that. They are original, imaginative and above all else - kind.

When I dreamt up this competition I thought I wanted to hear weird and wonderful acts of kindness. But when I read the stories in lockdown it was the normality I craved. The normal acts that really hit home and made me smile. Filling the dishwasher, playing with little brothers, helping hedgehogs, giving your little sister some of your bacon when the dog ate hers.

Normal Acts of Everyday Kindness. These are what define us.

Thank you to all our amazing authors for reminding us of that.

I would love to end with a quote from one of our stories now, because it would fit here perfectly, but I don't want to steal the author's line. Remember this when you read the last sentence of *"The Breathtaking Adventure,"* that would have been a great sentence to end my foreword!

Instead I'll end with an amazing poster that one of our charities "Cheesy Waffles" created during lockdown. I think this poster sums everything up better than I ever could.

Enjoy the stories.

Gilesgate Story Challenge 2020

First Place Winner

The Super Secret Society Of Kindness

By Noah Jack Hockey

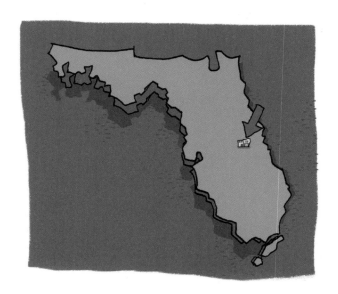

In a house far, far, far away... (No, I'm not talking about Star Wars)... Florida to be precise, it was 8.30am.

RINNNNNNNNNNGGGGGGG, Ruby's alarm clock went off at 'Super Duper Really loud alarm clock' mode.

One hour later (Yes – One. Whole. Hour.)

"Ugh!" Ruby exclaimed as she eventually turned off her annoying sleep interrupter. Lazy, right? As she stomped sleepily down the stairs, Ruby questioned herself, "Why, why, why do I have to get up so early?"

"Siiiiiiisssss," came a taunting voice from the dreaded recliner, "I'm going to get the TV controller and there's nothing you can do to stop me!"

"Noooooooo!!!" Ruby's little, lazy stomps immediately became speedy steps so she could swipe the remote, maybe even before Chloe moved a millimetre!

One minute later, Ruby and Chloe were battling like William the conqueror vs Alfred the Great!

(I'll admit that 'HADOUKEN' was crazy but true! It's because Chloe was addicted to Street Fighter 2).

What they didn't realise was that Dadums (their Father) watched the whole fight and rolled his eyes with each resounding specimen of onomatopoeia. "Errrrr... babe Errrr... the girls are Errrrr... fighting again!!!"

Serena muttered two words under her breath so bad I cannot tell you! Okay, if you insist, but you're in for a big shock, it was ' #%*(£ %$ £&*!'

YOU AT THE BACK, STOP CRYING, SHE WAS REALLY CROSS, O.K? IF YOU CARRY ON I'LL KICK YOU OUT OF THE BOOK CLUB!!!!!

Right, where were we?

Ah, yes, here.

"Holy mackerel wha' are you girls figh'ng over again?" asked Serena.

"CHLOE SLAPPED ME!!!" shouted Ruby, as if it was a big deal.

"SHE KICKED ME REALLY HARD!!!" argued Chloe, whingeing as loud as she could to get her parents to feel sorry her.

"B-E-D!!! BEEEEDDDD!!!!!" shouted Dadums after taking in a lot of air.

"Ugh, so lame." Chloe sulked as if her life wasn't fair.

"Meh, at least I'll get more sleep. Hooray!" Ruby exclaimed with a big, fat yaaaawwwwnnnn.

Moments later, Ruby tucked herself into bed, hugged her Bunny teddy and tried to drift off to sleep.

However, something was taking over her mind, she thought... she thought it was sorrow for Chloe! For a split second she couldn't believe this feeling overtook her brain! But it was true – she kind of, no, totally utterly absolutely felt sorry for her dear sister!

Meanwhile... Chloe was sulking her head off (Not literally, otherwise... R.I.P Chloe Williams). "I sure hope she's sulking as well, because she deserves it for being so mean." Chloe said, angrily.

But she calmed down eventually and said, "Actually, I'll take it back for once because that kick didn't hurt that much. And, I truly feel sorry for her, even if she doesn't want me to. RUBY!!! COME DOWN HERE!!!"

Tiptoe, tiptoe, went Ruby's feet as she tried not to be noticed by her parents. Seconds later, Ruby slipped into Chloe's room.

"I'm sorry Chloe," Ruby admitted.

"I'm sorry too, Ruby," Chloe said.

They gave each other a hug and, just like that, their fight was a distant memory!

Whispering, they hatched a plan to show Dadums and Serena that they were sorry too and could do better (let's be honest that wouldn't be hard given their previous form, would it?).

After a few minutes of *hard* work, this was their creation:

*Dearest Dadums and Serena, We're Super Duper
Mega Ultra Out Of This World sorry that we fought in
the living room. We're even more sorrier because we were
fighting over the stupid TV remote!
We are ever so sorry for today's mishap.
Love from
Ruby and Chloe*
xxxx   xxxx

"Let's go and give Serena and Dadums their sorry card, in secret,"
they agreed, sneaking along the corridor.

Minutes later...

"Placing card on the arm of the recliner, over," reported Chloe,
talking as if she was using a walkie-talkie.

"Shhhh Chloe. Tee hee hee," Ruby giggled, as she watched Chloe
sneakily insert the card into Dadums' hand while he was asleep.

*****

As luck would have it, the card had the desired effect on Serena and Dadums (even though Serena thought it was a wedding invitation and was momentarily unimpressed when she realised it wasn't).

The sisters felt a mushy feeling smack in the middle of their hearts which made them think of more kind things to do to unleash their mushiness onto the world, mwah, ha, ha, ha, haaaaaaa.

They named their new project:

THE SUPER SECRET SOCIETY OF KINDNESS!!!

On a weekly basis, they planned smooshy projects (The next one smooshier than the last).

Here are some of these mush-inducing moments:

- Knocking on the neighbours' doors and running away... hang on, that's naughty! Oh, wait, I missed one thing, they were leaving bouquets of flowers on their doorsteps.

- Filling Dadums' secret snack bar cupboard with empty crisp packets. Wait a minute, why would they want to do that? Oh, that's right, yes – they joined The Crisp Packet Project together and set to work making insulated, plastic-covered blankets for their street friends.

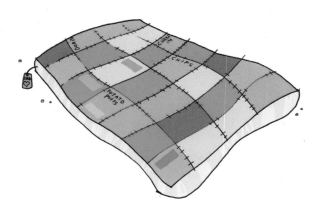

- Writing letters to absolute strangers – old ones at that. What? Really? Sounds like a stupid thing to do if you ask me! Ah, yes, they joined Postcards Of Kindness and wrote to nursing home residents all over the country (Ugh, I messed up again, I'm gonna get fired at this rate).

Before long, 'The Secret Society Of Kindness' was spreading it's mushy sensation to every corner of the world! Ruby and Chloe were global stars!!!

It turned out being kind was kind of – no, absolutely – cool. Who knew? (I did, clever me (smug expression)) That's not to say they didn't have a few arguments/scraps/fisticuffs occasionally. Usually over the controller of the TV.

Same old, same old; that's life people. But now, of course, they were so busy with their ruthless kindness that they didn't have time to be angry at each other for no exceptionally spectacular reason.

THE END
(almost)

90 Years Later...

———

Wibbling and wobbling, Chloe shuffled out into the garden, leaning precariously on her trusty zimmer frame. Ruby doddered behind her darling sister, clutching her walking stick for dear life.

"Are you thinking what I'm thinking?" Chloe croaked.

"Oh Yeah!!!" coughed Ruby, cursing herself. 98-year-old lungs were not designed for shouting.

"One more act of kindness. For old times' sake," they agreed.

Digging deep into the pockets of their pinnies, they both rummaged to find their original, only-two-ever-made, prized possession founding members of The Super Secret Society Of Kindness badges, and held them aloft. Still wibbling and wobbling, they hid them under a _____ to be found by future generations to carry on their legacy. '

A what?' I hear you cry. 'Please, we beg of you!'

Dear Readers, where those badges are, I cannot tell. However, if you choose kindness over silly spats, destiny might lead you to the location of the legendary badges of absolute kindness.

And as for Chloe and Ruby, moments after the badges left the extraordinary pair, a warm, mushy swirl of kindness wrapped itself around them and lifted them, smiling and giggling, off their feet to begin an everlasting life of kindness.

About Noah

Noah is a ten-year-old bookworm, who reads anything that stands still long enough! His story was inspired by acts of kindness featured on the local news, as well as frequent scraps with his sisters over the tv remote!

Both charities mentioned in his story are small, real charities that you can find on Facebook. Knocking on people's doors is not a charity but you can do it as long as you remember the flower bit.

Judges' Comments

A hilarious, witty tale with a strong and humorous narrative voice and a touching ending. This story had us laughing out loud, and smiling broadly. It left us with the fuzzy feeling inside that Chloe and Ruby spent their lives giving others – absolutely superb!

Second Place Winner

The Breathtaking Adventure

———————

———————

By Adrianna King

Chapter One

Once upon a dream there lived an enchanted forest.

You have never seen a forest so beautiful as this one. It had flowers that smelled like the strongest, sweetest perfume that your nostrils can imagine, and a river that shimmers like pearls runs through it. The trees waved like graceful swans dancing in the breeze. In this enchanted forest lived, among the other magical creatures, the fairies. For many years the Queen Fairy had been the ruler of all fairies and creatures, and they loved her because she ruled with kindness. They all lived happily in the forest, all because of the spell...

"Rainbows and sparkles and a dash of love,

Protects us all on the ground and above."

This spell was created by the Royal fairy ancestors to keep everyone in the Kingdom safe, and all the fairies in the forest were taught the spell from a young age. The fairies needed the spell because they had been under threat for a long time. Their enemies were evil scientists, who wanted the fairies' magic to make them more powerful.

One day, the evil scientists attacked the forest with so much force that they broke through the rainbow spell. They took the queen and trapped her in their laboratory headquarters at the top of the forbidden mountain that lay just beyond the enchanted forest, and prepared to do experiments on her to extract the ultimate fairy magic. The queen was afraid, but more than that, she was disappointed— disappointed because she felt like she had let all of her people down and failed to protect the kingdom....

Chapter Two

It was many years later, and outside of the enchanted forest people did not believe in magic anymore — they didn't even believe in fairies.

The forest was still magical, but without the power of its Fairy queen and the belief of the outside world, its magic was fading fast.

One day, for the first time in many years, a child entered the forest. She was named Coco. She was an expert gymnast — that was how she managed to penetrate the magical forcefield that still protected the fairy kingdom. She leapt through the trees at so much speed that she broke through the spell.

She saw all of the fairies and creatures that were suffering as their magic faded. They were suffering because, after many years of terrible torture at the hands of the evil scientists, their Queen was losing her magical powers. The creatures of the kingdom could not live without their magic, and if their Queen died,

then they all would too, and the beautiful enchanted forest would belong to the evil scientists who were still trying to extract the magic that they didn't deserve to have.

When Coco entered the forest, at first the fairies were afraid, but when they knew that she meant them no harm, they told Coco about their suffering. She was horrified, and agreed to help them. Coco knew just what to do to help them survive – her mum was a vet, and she had always paid close attention to her mum's work. That evening, she raced home and gathered all of the important items that she knew she would need. She stumbled back into the forest as quickly as she could, leaping through the magical forcefield that was growing weaker by the day.

Coco told the fairies she was ready to do whatever it took to help them. They were so grateful they shed tears of beautiful crystal.

They asked Coco why she was risking everything to help them.

She replied "I am helping you because I don't want to live in a world without magic."

The fairies wept again, amazed at the kindness of this wonderful human.

Then suddenly, when Coco was about to begin her adventure, a fairy flew forward and said bravely "I volunteer to help."

The fairy was very important, and her name was Luna. She was beautiful. She had brown eyes that shimmered. Her tanned skin glowed like the sunset. Luna had crystal wings that shined like a diamond. Her dress smelled like ripe, perfect grapes.

"The Queen is my mother," said Luna. "I must come too!"

"Okay," said Coco. "Together we are stronger!" And so they set off towards the laboratories, not knowing what was going to happen.

Chapter Three

Coco and Luna began climbing up the mountain that lay beyond the forest. Eventually they got somewhere close to the top. Then, they realised it was getting too dark to go any further. They put up a tent, got their sleeping bags out and three, two one…. They were asleep!

Zzzzzzzzzzz...

The next morning, the sun began to rise in the sky. Then it was officially morning. Coco said "what a beautiful sunrise". Luna woke up slowly and admired the sunrise with Coco.

They were so distracted by the beauty around them, that they didn't realise that they were being surrounded by the huge ogres that lived on the mountain. The ogres didn't like strangers, and were known for being grumpy! The head ogre bellowed "Who goes there?" and his voice sounded like thunder. Coco and Luna jumped up with a fright. When the head ogre saw them, he cried "How dare you trespass on our mountain? Get off now!" Coco was trying to think fast. They didn't want to give up now. Then she remembered – kindness goes a long way. She searched in the tent for something to show the ogre some kindness.

Before long she found a bag of peaches that they had freshly picked from the enchanted forest before they had left on their journey. Trembling, Coco held out the bag to the ogres and said "I'm so sorry that we have disturbed you. Please forgive us. We don't mean any harm. We are on an important journey to rescue the Fairy Queen of the enchanted forest. Would you accept these beautiful sweet peaches from us as a gift to say sorry?"

The head ogre was silent for a moment. Slowly, he reached out his long hairy hand and took the bag of peaches. Without saying anything, he bit into one slowly.

Coco and Luna watched him nervously.

Suddenly, a big smile spread across his face. He gave the bag of peaches to the rest of the ogres. They all took one, and then they all smiled too as the sweet juices ran down their chins. "Thank you very much," said the ogres. "We appreciate your kindness. We have grown suspicious of strangers since the strange men came. You may now continue your journey."

Coco thought for a moment, and then said "Strangers? Can you describe them?"

The ogres described men with machines that made terrible noises.

The head ogre pointed to the top of the mountain. "That is where they are. It is not safe to go there."

Coco replied "We have no choice."

The ogres nodded, and moved so that Coco could continue on her journey, with Luna buzzing along beside her.

Chapter Four

Gradually, they made their way to the tip-top of the mountain, where grey mist swirled around mysteriously. Coco could feel something in the air change. She knew that Luna could feel it too. They both had a bad feeling deep inside. It was a feeling that someone else was close by, like they were being watched. There were strange noises getting louder and louder the further they walked. It sounded like an animal, but not one Coco had ever heard before. As the mist cleared, gradually they were able to see where the noise was coming from. It was a fierce and bold dragon, guarding the entrance to the laboratory buildings. The dragon looked at them with beady eyes. He opened his mouth and for one terrible moment Coco and Luna thought they were toast. Instead of breathing fire on them though, the dragon let out a long, loud cry "ooooowwwwww!!!!" He started to flap his wing as his side. "What is the matter?" Asked Coco.

"Go away – you shouldn't be here," said the dragon. He sounded angry, but in pain as well.

"Please, let me help you," Said Coco.

"You can't help me!" The dragon cried. "No one can." And then he turned around and sobbed.

"Please let me try," said Coco. Slowly, the dragon turned around and showed Coco his wing. She could see that his wing had heavy chains tied to them, and the chains were cutting through his skin.

She realised that the scientists were making the dragon guard their laboratories by keeping him prisoner.

"Maybe I can help?" Luna asked, flying forward gently. I know a healing spell. The dragon looked up. "You can do magic?" He asked. "A little," said Luna. It isn't as strong as it used to be. She flew over to the dragon's wing and gently pressed her hands on it. Then she sang.

"Healing hands show the way, so you can live another day." Nothing seemed to happen, no matter how many times Luna said the spell. Luna was exhausted and she fell to the floor sobbing. "It's no good. My magic is fading. We don't have long left." Coco thought hard and then looked in her bag. She took out one of the tools she had taken from her dad's toolbox and started to work on breaking the chains on the dragon's wing. After lots of sweating, finally they were amazed to see the heavy chains fall away onto the floor. The dragon cried tears of happiness. He told them all about how the evil scientists had put him in chains and forced him to guard their laboratory. He agreed to help them.

The dragon blew flaming red hot fire. Through the middle of it was a clear path for them to travel down. As the

38

fire got warmer, the girls got closer to the huge steel laboratory door. They stood back as the dragon breathed a terrible gust of flames that burned down the door. Coco dodged the hot sparks that flew through the air. Now that the door was gone, a loud siren began to go off. They didn't have much time. Looking around, Coco saw the Queen sitting sadly in a tiny cage looking very weak. They raced over. What Coco did not realise was that there was an evil scientist behind her. Coco reached out to the cage and grabbed the queen. The evil scientist behind her laughed. "You're too late!" He said. "She is no good to us now. We might not have been able to use her magic, but she doesn't have any left either." The fairy queen looked up sadly and said "It is true. We are all doomed."

The dragon came in and breathed even more fire around. It created a flamey path that the scientists could not cross. Coco and the fairies raced outside with the dragon. He thanked them for their kindness and flew away.

He was finally free.

Chapter Five

The Queen was very weak, so Coco carried her very gently all the way back down the mountain and into the forest in the palm of her hand. The Queen wept and so did Luna. They explained to Coco that without their magic, the enchanted forest would not survive much longer. Coco couldn't help but cry. "I'm so sorry" she said. I wanted to help you because I didn't want to live in a world without magic, and I have failed."

But when they got back to the forest, instead of seeing everyone weak and fading, the fairies and creatures looked healthy and happy. They were full of joy to see their Queen.

"I don't understand" said Luna. "Neither do I" said Coco. The fairy Queen was very quiet and thoughtful as she looked around carefully. Then she turned to Coco.

"Now I understand." She said "You saved me and my people today, with all of your kind acts. You said you don't want to live in a world without magic. But kindness is a form of magic, and as long as there is kindness in the world, then magic will never die."

About Adrianna

I love to make up stories and I'm especially interested in magical creatures like fairies and unicorns. I sometimes wonder if they really exist and I hope they do! I wanted to show in my story that magic is possible for everyone in your own way.

Judges' comments

A beautifully imagined story with a powerful and moving twist that had one of our judges close to tears, and made our imaginations soar. Excellent!

Gilesgate Story Challenge 2020

Vicki's Favourite

Armageddon Protocol

By Dan Baker

The Year is 4,001.

You might be imagining vast, futuristic cities where it was more likely that you owned a spaceship than a car.

But no.

In place of giant cities where great nations live, smoking ruins lie. Skyscrapers toppled. Mansions shattered. Houses crumbled. If you are wondering what could cause such devastation, then I will tell you: Armageddon Protocol. A computer virus that can turn any robot against humans. As you can imagine, humans were relying on robots more and more every day. this meant that computer viruses were very dangerous, especially such large-scale viruses as this one. This is the story of a 10 year-old boy who has been forced to live through this crisis:

Jack shrank into the shadows. He didn't dare to breathe. He knew that if he moved so much as a muscle, he would be caught and brutally murdered. He had to get back to his hideout or he would never see daylight again (it was generally safer to scavenge at night as the robot's sensors were hindered by the darkness). He waited until the scanner had passed over (and missed) him, he clambered onto the roof of a house and was away.

Back at his secret headquarters, Jack scraped himself a meagre meal and prepared to rest for the day to prepare himself for the next night's adventure (Jack had become partially nocturnal because in was easy to choose between the relative safety of the darkness and the all-revealing glow of the sun). All of a sudden, a piercing scream punctured the night air. He leapt to his feet. If he tried to save the person who was in trouble, it would be putting himself at great risk, but if he didn't... He cast away the thought and raced out into the night.

As Jack hurtled over the rooftops, he looked at the wreckage strewn across the city. There was Durham Cathedral, with its tall proud towers lying on the long strip of once-green grass that was palace green. Durham Castle, too, was looking like so many other medieval castles. When Jack finally reached what he thought was the source of the screaming, he saw the reason why instantly. Construction droids. They were the robots that had had access to laser cutters and chainsaws before they were taken over. They were also extremely powerful, which made them formidable foes. Jack knew that he would have to fight. He grabbed a disused laser cutter and sliced clean through the nearest robot to him. Unfortunately, this alerted every other robot in the vicinity. Now for the hard part. Jack sprinted over to nearby crane and proceeded to hack through the base of it. After what seemed like eternity, the crane gave one last groan and toppled onto the rest of the robots. As soon as he was sure that there weren't any more lurking in the shadows, Jack ran over to the pile of chains that the robots had been gathered around. Hoping that it wasn't too late, he slashed through them. They fell away to reveal a young boy around the same age as Jack.

"Thank you," he said, "You saved me."

After that,they became the best of friends, and, although the robots did not stop attacking, they still had each other.

The End

About Dan

Dan likes to read every book he can get his hands on and loves to bake delicious treats. He spends his spare time with his brothers, making origami and eating the delicious treats he has made.

Judges' Comments

You know that you've found a special story when you're hooked within the first three lines.

'But no.'

That's what did it for me.

You think you know what this tale is going to be like, reader? Guess again.

Brilliant. And what follows is drama and excitement, wrapped in an engaging concept and set against the backdrop of an eerie post-apocalyptic Durham.

I enjoyed every bit of it - and would love to join Jack and his friend on their new adventures!

Miles' favourite

The Wolf Whisperer

By Evie Turner

Chapter One
The saviour

"JADE!!!!!" Screamed Jade's mum.

"I'm coming," Jade moaned as she slouched down the stairs. She had got given A LOT of homework from Mrs Anderson; Jade was very tired from all the assignments she was given.

Jade's mum sighed and then spoke, "Will you go to the town and deliver this note to the post office please?"

Jade snatched the note from her mum's hand and threw her coat on. "Gladly," Jade said, "Anything to get away from home-work."

As Jade walked across the cobblestone path, through the woods, she was curious as to what was in the note. Jade looked down at the letter, deciding whether she should open the note or not, but she didn't notice that she walked off the path. When Jade finally decided to look up and leave the note, she was lost. Jade looked around trying to find the path, it was nowhere to be seen. She turned around suddenly and saw a bear glaring back at her. Jade screamed running for dear life. She heard the mighty roars of the bear behind but tripped on a root and twisted her ankle.

"OUCH," Jade shrieked. The bear came towering over her. "Is this the end?" Jade thought. A wolf howled as it pounced on top of the bear attacking it. Jade stood back. When the fight was over, and the wolf whimpered and limped over to Jade with a bleeding paw. "Aw you poor thing, here this should stop the bleeding." Jade wrapped a spare bandage she had in her leather bag around the wolf's wound and stroked its head.

"Th-thanks." The wolf muttered.

Jade blinked blankly, "What?"

Chapter Two
The Necklace

——————

"Thanks," Muttered the wolf once more, "You're a really kind girl Jade, I could see it in your eyes."

"Uh, how am I talking to a wolf?" Jade questioned looking down into the wolf's deep blue eyes.

The wolf laughed and said, "Haven't you noticed? Look down."

Jade was confused but did as she was told and looked down. "Huh, why is my necklace glowing!?" Jade questioned the wolf.

"Well," The wolf started, "You are talking to me, a wolf."

"Right...." Jade said.

The wolf carried on, "That necklace is magical, it was created by the first human and wolf who became one with each other, and that created a constellation."

"That's SOOOOO cool!" Jade stated, still looking down at the necklace.

"Every one to five years the next alpha wolf will howl to the moon at midnight to go on a mission with his human friend to keep the constellation in the sky." The wolf explained, then sighed, "But, if they don't accomplish the mission in time, the constellation will fade away."

"Oh no," Jade said. Her and the wolf lay there beside an oak tree talking and Jade even helped the wolf walk with its hurt paw.

When Jade was called in from her mother, she told her what happened with the wolf and her mum explained that it runs in the family. "So, can I go and see the wolf again?" Jade questioned her mother with a mouthful of spaghetti in her mouth.

"Ok then Jade but be back by 8:00." Jade's mother answered back.

"Ok I will," Jade said excitedly, "Bye mum!"

As she walked through the woods, Jade was looking down at the magical necklace, wondering if it could possibly have any other powers.

Chapter Three
Trustworthy Friends

———————

"Hey Jade!" Said Blake, Jade's friend.

"What are you doing?" Asked Selene, who was also Jade's friend.

"Oh nothing, just looking for something," She said. Jade walked along the path, unaware that her curious friends where following her. Finally, she found her furry friend, the wolf.

"Hey," Jade said as the wolf lay on her lap, "Do you have a name?"

"No," The wolf answered back looking up at her.

Jade got excited and started to come up with names, but the wolf could smell something, humans. He rose from Jade's lap and started to sniff out the smell.

"AGH" Jade's friends screamed, "PLEASE, DON'T HURT US!"

Jade walked over and sighed, "Chill guys, this is my friend, he won't hurt you."

"What's his name?" Selene asked in interest.

"His name, his name," Jade muttered, "His name is, VENUS!"

Venus the wolf pounced around; he loved his name. Jade

even translated some of the things Venus said for them.

"Guys," Jade said to Blake and Selene, "Can I trust you guys to keep this secret, cause I'm sure my mum won't be too happy that you found out about this."

"Of course, you can trust us!" Blake said assuring he and Selene would keep this secret.

"Thanks!" Jade said, "I can really trust you guys."

She ran off into the distance heading for home, prepared for what could possibly happen the next day.

Chapter Four
The Midnight Howl

Jade awoke at twilight, to see the whole moon almost above her head. Suddenly, she heard a howl echoing through her ear, and recognized it, Venus! Jade went running to her wolf friend in the darkness of the night. She found him in a sad mood. "What's the matter?" Jade asked Venus.

"The constellation, it's fading," Venus began, then turned to Jade, "I believe our mission has begun."

Jade looked startled but in a determined voice said I'm ready.

Jade and Venus started to set off on their journey starting under the constellation. Before they set off for the long journey the two friends said goodbye to their parents.

"I'll miss you guys," Said Jade, "I love you."

"We love you to," Said Jade's dad, "Now go and accomplish this Journey to save the constellation."

So, she did, Jade went off to find Venus.

"Be careful son," Venus' father warned him, "When me and Jade's father went on this Journey it was tougher than we thought."

"I will dad, I love you guys." Said Venus flopping his ears down.

Jade and Venus met up and headed to the rock where the moon and the constellation was. They waited there for some time then the first star of the constellation shone down on the rock and revealed a rhyme to give them a clue for their first task. All the tasks were not only to keep the constellation in the sky, but to test their friendship for one another.

Jade read out the first rhyme,
Your first task is rocky,
Quite easy to one,
But don't get to cocky,
Try and test your Loyalty.

Jade and Venus looked at each other and knew where to go, "Shipwreck Bay!" They both cheered.

Chapter Five
Loyalty

———————

Jade and Venus walked along the path heading towards Shipwreck Bay. You see, the Boulder Beach was infamous for being haunted by the ghost of Grey May. She was a lady pirate who died from a shipwreck because of her enemy Blackjack. They say after she died her treasure was buried on this beach. No one dared to go there after someone was found dead at the cliffs of this beach. People say it was the ghost of Grey May who pushed him off.

"Here we are," Muttered Jade, "Shipwreck Bay."

"Oh, come on! What's the worst that can happen?" said Venus. He climbed up some of the rocks and said, "Let's go Jade, we haven't got much time until the constellation fades."

Jade took a deep breath and began to climb. The rocks were quite loose, but Venus managed to get to the top of the cliff.

"I'll start looking up here Jade," Venus shouted down to Jade, who was barley up.

She looks like she needs some help, Venus thought to himself.

"Good idea Venus!" Shouted Jade," I'm fine, carry on."

He did as Jade insisted and carried on looking. A while later, Venus sniffed out something, a chest! It had a piece of thin paper on it with the next clue. Venus got very curious and decided to look in the chest and found some gold coins.

"AHHH!" Screamed a voice. Venus jumped then looked down the cliff, it was Jade.

"VENUS HELP I'M GONNA FALL!" she shouted as more rocks began to crumble. Venus looked at Jade in shock unaware of what to do. He looked at the treasure, it was fading. Venus ran as fast as he could to the treasure and grabbed the note. Jade was holding onto a tiny ledge; it was a long fall. The ledge crumbled.

"JADE GRAB ONTO MY PAW!" Venus said reaching his paw down to Jade. Without a flinch, Jade gripped onto Venus' paw as he dragged her up to safety.

Jade took a big sigh of relief and hugged Venus, "You saved my life, thank you."

They both looked at the note and read the next clue,

Well done you've finished the first task,
It was quite tempting,
Your next one involves a lot of rust
But you cannot be scared,
For one must trust.

Chapter Six
Trust

Jade and Venus knew they needed to go to the Rust Junk Yard so that's where they headed. It took a while, but they got there in the end.

This task they already knew involved a treasure hunt. They needed to search for the right treasure, which was a gold coin with the constellation on it.

"Found anything?" Questioned Jade.

"Nope," Said Venus sniffing in all places.

Jade began to climb a hill of rusty cars. Venus followed her; he was picking up a scent. Suddenly, Venus slipped and was hanging from the rusty hill. Jade was already at the top but heard Venus' howl. Jade was startled, she looked around for something that could help, then saw it.

"Venus," She shouted," Let go."

"What!?" Venus said shocked," No it's too dangerous."

"You need to trust me." Jade answered smiling at Venus. He did and let go of the edge.

Jade had seen an old soft mattress below Venus and she it would give him a soft landing.

"Jade!" He shouted up," I've found the coin!"

Jade climbed down in excitement as the coin started to

glow. It turned into their last clue! Jade and Venus read it out in their heads. They both knew they needed to go to the dry lakes.

Chapter Seven
The Creator's Gift

———————

Finally Jade and Venus arrived at the lake and walked along the dry sand path leading to the top.

"We must hurry Jade!" Venus said, "We haven't got much time."

Jade looked at the constellation, it was almost faded.

Venus and Jade started to run and finally were there at the top. They investigated the deep night sky hoping something might happen, and it did. The constellation began to glow shinning brighter than before. Two giant ghosts shone down on them, a wolf and a human.

"The first human and wolf to become best friends!" Jade and Venus said together.

"Thank you," The human ghost said.

"Once again we can have another five years go by with human and wolf in harmony," said the wolf.

Jade and Venus bowed down to the gods. Jade and Venus had their necklaces removed and they sadly looked at each other.

The gods couldn't help but feel sorry for them, so they gave them both a gift, another necklace! This way the two friends could keep talking and being friends forever.

"Thank you so much!" Jade and Venus said, glad that they would be able to remain friends forever. Thanks to the Creator's gift.

Chapter Eight
Home With You

———————

Jade and Venus began to walk home looking up at the beautiful shining constellation glad they were able to save it for five more years.

The next day Jade and Venus spent time together and so did their parents. At the end of the day Jade and Venus decided they would go star gazing and it was a good idea! It turned into like a camping trip. Jade and Venus loved having each other's company and spent a lot of time together.

"Good to be home," Venus said.

"Yeah, especially since I can spend it with you." Jade said back huddling up with Venus as they both drifted off to sleep with the constellation shining down overhead.

About Evie

Hi, I'm Evie the author of The Wolf Whisperer. When I heard about this competition I thought it would be a nice idea to write my own story.

I had a lot of fun writing it and didn't expect for it to get published. Even though I didn't win the main category, I am still glad my story is going to be in a book. Most of all, it was a great experience writing it and it's a great inspiration to write books and show your creativity.

Judges' Comments

I've always been a huge fan of nature and animal stories, especially those which show our hero's connection with the natural world. The Wolf Whisperer did a wonderful job of establishing this fantastical friendship.

Simon's Favourite

The Llama Who Lost His Smile

By Zoe

There once was a llama called Carl but one day his life got turned upside down. That's when he lost his smile.

What was a llama to do with no smile. Normally he would go into town and give soup to the unfortunate hungry community and see the smile on their faces, but it wasn't the soup that made the people so happy, it was the smile on Carls face and his comforting voice telling them it was going to be okay.

Carl with nothing to do decided to go on a walk and cheer himself up. As he got ready for the walk, a postcard with the cutest dog carl had ever seen fell on the floor. Carl picked it up and read the back of it.

It said "go to the village hall at 4:30am", that was only 20 minutes from now. He thought he would go however, first he would put on his best hat, the one with the red lace.

On his walk to the village hall he saw an injured bird, without thinking he picked it up and helped it fly up to it's mother nest. Now Carl was 3 minutes late but it was worth it.

Carl eventually got to the village hall and there was pink and blue balloons all over. His heart started beating faster and faster. He was scared but he knew it was only nerves so with his heart thumping he pushed open the door and with a great surprise it was all the town, with big smiling faces. Carl just stood there stiff, shocked for about one moment or two until, a little girl said, "This is a thank you gift for your kindness over the years".

"Yeah like when you found my dog by making a hotdog trail to my house", shouted a woman.

"And when you helped me move house," called out a man.

"You have all helped us but we have never thanked you properly so hear it!"

"Thank you", shouted everyone.

That's when Carls face changed, a big grin from ear to ear. And he was the happiest llama in the world. His kindness had earned him the best reward ever, good friends with smiling faces, just like him.

Judges' Comments

Fun and thoughtful, this story oozes whimsy and charm, and on reading it, reminded us quite strongly of the works of Doctor Seuss. Carl is such a wonderful character and the world needs more people like him.

Best Lockdown Story

The Story that is Neverending

By Lucy-Jo Patten

This is where my story starts.

It was just an ordinary day and I thought my day was going brilliant but then my parents had got an email from school. I thought it would just be about any random thing but I was wrong. It was about my school closing because of a virus.

Many people were scared and didn't know what was going to happen next. I wondered if I would ever go back and questioned constantly what is going to happen to me and the rest of the world? This virus was breaking the country everyone didn't know what was going to happen next and there were daily meetings to see where we stand with this virus.

The one thing I said was "it doesn't matter what they say people are going to ignore it anyway."

I was right... people were ignoring the rules that had been put in place to stop the spread. I guess people have their own way of going through this time. Shops were running out of supplies and if you had toilet roll you were very lucky to get it. People rushing to shops to stock pile and weren't even thinking about the elderly that can't get to the shops immediately and worrying if they could even leave their homes. Selfish is a word I would describe those that didn't think before they took the supplies that the most vulnerable people needed.

The next stage was what is going to happen now?

They stopped people over the age of 70 going out their homes even if they didn't have the essentials they need. They would now have to deal with what they could get until further notice. I questioned to myself who and what is going to help them. This is where the country was beginning to come together, volunteers coming across the globe to help those most vulnerable. Getting the essentials, they would travel to the moon and back if they had to get the supplies that they needed. People were becoming more familiar with what was happening around them. People travelling home with a truck load of electronics so they can still work and be able to pay the bills for their family.

People trying to keep to the rules of social distancing but there was some that didn't care if they could have spread the virus to them. People working hard to stop the virus making sure we stay home and stay safe. But that wasn't the case not everyone was safe especially the people that still had to keep working and risk their lives for everyone else. They were the true workers fighting to keep our country safe and the people that lived in it.

My first week of being off school was fine I had a lot of work set but it wasn't like normal school. I had finished my work so quickly and I had all this free time I didn't know what to do and after a while it started to get boring. I was constantly on my phone doing literally nothing and I really didn't want to do this forever, so I needed to do something to change my situation.

So, I started to do a daily activity to keep me busy, while in the meantime there were people still working and making sure that our country was to stay safe and people were to stop as many people were getting ill, but no one was quite sure what would happen if it was to kill thousands of people in only a couple of months. People were starting to worry and trying to stay at home and only go out if needed. This is where it all started to change, rule after rule was put in place to try keep us safe. No one wanted to follow these rules but it was and is the only way we could get out of this pandemic.

It was the second week of this crazy outrage of a virus, people rushing off to shops to see if there was anything left for them or to have to go back home for an endless journey just to get some food. Queues going for miles even if you were to just get some milk. There was no time left for anything, people were spending just too much time queuing and there was no time for anything else. Only 5,10,15,1 person in a shop at any one time, the world was just going CRAZY! This is when the announcement was made that we were officially in lockdown and non-essential shops were closed and would not be open until the foreseeable future.

People were trying to rush to the shops before they closed for good and then there would nothing that they could do about it even if they queued for hours they might be turned around and told to go home. People were starting to hit the bottom of the world and realise what was happening. They could no longer meet their friends or family. They were told to stay at home and only go out if needed and try not come into contact with anyone. This meant anyone, even if it was your parents. Even if you didn't live with them you couldn't and wouldn't be able to see them until this whole situation was vanished. People were in tears not knowing if they could see their loved ones ever again.

This is my third week I don't know what is happening, I don't know if my family is okay and especially don't know if this will ever end. We are no longer to go out as a family to a shop. Only 1 person from your house is allowed to go out to shop for essentials. People are scared and so am I, about that one person that is going out for essentials if they come back and have caught this deadly and horrible virus!

People will never know if it will ever be the same again. There are many decisions made that are risky for those and this is why I would like to thank those that are doing the most to protect us and our country.

Thank you for NHS you are the most important you have been risking your own lives to save ours. Thank you to the PM you are delivering news to the world to keep us safe and telling us what is happening and answering questions that are being asked all over the globe. Thank you to the Police that are making sure only those that need to be going out are going out, and those that are not following the rules to be told and learn that they could be affecting everyone else's lives. Thank you to the world, we may have some rough times but you are always here no matter what and nothing can change that.

There is never going to be an end to this world so it is just a goodbye for now and hope to see you again soon fellow reader.

Life is short or long but the world will always bring everyone together, as it can be and is possible if we all work together. People may be different but who isn't? It doesn't matter who you are or where you are from this world is just one big family and you should be proud to be in it.

The world has gone through problems causing the passes of many vulnerable lives but we can get through this together and no one can or will break the way that happens. Just make sure to stay safe and stay well!

My act of kindness was to make sure my family was okay and it was and is always my main priority. Even if the world was at an edge I would always put my family first over anything and everything!

About Lucy-Jo

Hi I'm Lucy-Jo, but you can call me LJ! This is my story of what happened whilst we were in lockdown.

Are we still in it and how are you?

I hope you're good! This book was inspired to show what is happening in our world. This is also to make sure we remember not just the present but the past too! I hope you enjoy reading my story as it is little bit weird to be thinking of what has/had been happening!

Most Emotional Story

The Kindest Thing That Happened to Me

By Chadhed Allouch

The most kindest thing that have ever happened to me was when we were in Syria (my country).

My mom was the only one to take care of me and my 3 brothers and 2 of them were still babies. My dad wasn't with us because he was trying to get our paper work so we can move countries. My mom was really tired so my aunties come to our house so they looky after me and my brother but then there was a bomb in our house. My baby brother was about to die. Me and my other 2 brothers were ok but lots of glass came in our faces(you can still see the marks on my brothers face).

For my aunt the wall fell on her, but some people saw what happened and came running to help us. Some of my dads friends took us to the hospital and some let us stay at their house although its really small and my mom forced her life for us so without those people I don't know what would've happened to us.

Most Raised For Charity

Watson's Daily Walk

By Oliver Wilson

Chapter One

Watson lived happily with his two humans, Norman and Claire. The three of them were a family and Watson loved being with them. Sometimes he did wish there was another dog in the house to keep him company but he thought, you can't have everything.

"Watson! Come here boy! Walkies." Watson, the daschund and his owner, Norman, were going on their daily walk to the park. When Watson heard his owner call he ran straight into the kitchen where Norman was ready to put his harness onto him. He sat and Norman knelt and put the harness on him. They walked to the door, opened it and stepped outside into the world.

When they got to the park, Watson ran towards another dog, his mate Ben. Ben was so happy to see him, he sniffed Watson's bum to say hello and wagged his tail. Watson did the same back. Norman, and Ben's owner, Abigail, sat on a bench and started chatting while the two dogs were chasing bees and rabbits and running through the meadow.

About half an hour later, Norman called for Watson and Abigail called for Ben. Norman clipped the lead onto Watson's harness and they set off back home.

When they got back Watson had his tea, kibble and dog meat. He finished that and went to bed. As he lay down he thought I wish I had a friend here to keep me company.

Chapter Two

———

The next day, Watson woke up bright and early and jumped on Claire and Norman's bed. He wanted to go on another walk to see Ben again. "Watson, it's only 6:00am!" Claire said, firmly. "Go back to bed!" Watson was very disappointed. He really wanted to go on a walk but he had to wait…

8:00am! Watson raced back into his owner's bedroom and started jumping on the bed again! Norman and Claire got out of bed, put on their dressing gowns and marched down the stairs. "After breakfast, we'll go on a walk. Ok Watson?"

"Woof!" Watson had some breakfast and so did his owners. Everyone got changed. Watson got his harness and lead put on. This time, Claire was coming too. She never normally came but she wanted to feel some fresh air.

Off the three of them went. Watson was happily pulling on the lead as he couldn't wait to get to the park to see Ben.

Chapter Three

Watson, Claire and Norman all got to the park. Watson could see Ben! He raced over to see him "Woof (Hi!)" Watson said.

"Woof woof! (Hi Watson!)" Ben replied.

"Hi, Norman and hi Claire, nice to see you again." Abigail said. The three of them started chatting.

Meanwhile, Watson and Ben were searching through the bins to try and find food. It was their hobby even though they weren't meant to do it! They found mouldy cheese, ice cream, fish and chips and even some sweets.

When Watson went into one of the bins he heard a rustling sound and faint whining and barking. As he searched the bin, he found a big blue bag. He dragged it out very carefully and opened it up. Inside were... Three little puppies! Ben howled for his owner and Watson ran over to the bench where they were all sitting. He pulled on Claire's dress to try and say there was something over there. She went with him and when she saw the puppies, her jaw dropped. "Norman! Come 'ere! Puppies!"

"Where, where?" Norman asked.

"In the bag! They're so cute!" Claire replied. "Shall we take them back home?"

"I think we should. They're biting my hand as if it's food!" Abigail heard all of the racket and went over. "What's going on?" Abigail asked.

"We've found puppies!" Claire said back.

"Awww, they're so cute."

"I know, aren't they just? We better take these little pups back home and feed them. See you later, Abigail." Claire said.

"See ya." Watson, Claire, Norman and the three pups went back home.

Chapter Four

Watson, Norman, Claire and the three girl pups who were now named Jessie, Lucy and Fluffy arrived home safely. Norman said they were around 8 weeks old.

Claire fed the pups. Norman put a blanket and some pillows out for them to sleep on, and Watson was just lying down in his bed. When the pups had been fed, instead of going over to the blanket and pillows to sleep on, they went over to Watson's bed and climbed in! Watson was annoyed. He was just drifting off when an army of pups came and raided his safe place! So Watson had to go over and sleep on the uncomfortable floor beside them. All 4 of them eventually went to sleep.

At about two o'clock in the morning, Norman and Claire both woke up to the 3 pups crying. They both rushed downstairs to see what the matter was. The pups were scared. Not just scared, very scared! It was their first night in the house and they just weren't used to it. Norman and Claire decided to sleep next to them on the floor as a comfort.

In the morning, Jessie woke up first. She went over to Watson and snuggled into him as if he was her dad. When Fluffy and Lucy woke up they did the same thing. Norman and Claire were so happy to see that the puppies loved Watson.

Chapter Five

Today was the day that Norman put Jessie, Lucy and Fluffy on PuppyGram! PuppyGram was a website where you could show off your dogs and ask for donations. Norman wasn't really wanting donations, he just wanted to see what people thought of the three puppies. After all, they were very cute. Norman went over to the pups, took a photo and walked over to his study. He uploaded the picture to the website and waited for responses.

About 2 hours later, Norman loaded up PuppyGram. His jaw dropped when he saw how many likes and comments he had got. He had 72,000 likes and 57,000 comments. Norman scrolled through the comments. People were saying "I'll give you 10 quid to help feed them!" So Norman put his bank account details onto the site for people to pay money into.

"Awww, they're so cute! Wish I had dogs like that!"

"Here's £20 for them. Buy them something nice." Norman was so happy, he could barely speak!

After he had looked at the comments he clicked on his bank account. At first he had £145 but now he had £960! He was amazed.

Chapter Six

———————

Seeing as Norman had hundreds of pounds in his bank account, he thought he should go and get some treats, toys and maybe a new bed for the 4 dogs who were living in his house. He drove to the pet shop, went in, went over to the dog section and picked out a lovely selection of things for the dogs. He bought the biggest dog bed they had, a kennel, some toys, a few treats and a lot of dog food. Norman walked over to the checkout, got out his card and paid £472.99 for all of the things he had bought.

As he was driving back home, he was thinking of how happy the dogs would be when he showed them the bed, treats and kennel.

Chapter Seven

When Norman got home there was a car outside his house. Norman had never seen it before. There were two people in his house and they introduced themselves as Tom and Sue from a local newspaper. They had been told about Norman and Claire's act of kindness and wanted to write about it. They took a lot of photos and Norman gave them all the details of how Watson had found the puppies and how they had looked after them.

The newspaper published a full page spread about Watson and the puppies. There were a lot of people who got in touch with the newspaper about the puppies. Over 200 people asked if they could have a puppy.

Norman, Claire and Watson won an award for their 'Act of Kindness' and were on TV. Even the Queen and Paul O'Grady sent them best wishes.

Chapter Eight

Watson was SO very happy. Norman and Claire decided that they couldn't let the puppies go to new homes so they kept them. Norman had 3 new friends with him all the time. He did have to tell them off sometimes but he really loved them. All four snuggled up together in the really big dog bed Norman had bought. The rest of the money that had been donated for the puppies was given to a Dog Rescue Centre. People all over the world kept asking about the puppies so Norman set up their own web page and any donations were given to dogs homes.

The puppies were growing and were full of life and energy. Everybody loved them. Norman had a calendar printed every year and it had photos of all four dogs on it. All the money raised from that went to Battersea Dogs Home.

Norman and Claire's one act of kindness had really set the ball rolling and in the end the puppies and Watson became stars. You never really know what one random act of kindness can do.

About Oliver

I have always liked writing stories and I really love dogs, My mum says I am dog mad, everything I buy is dog related. So I enjoy putting the two together.

I enjoy watching Paul O'Grady's 'For the love of dogs' and decided to write a book to raise money for Battersea dogs and cats home. I raised just over £170 selling them to family and friends. I choose to write my stories about a dog called Watson as my favourite breed of dog is the Dachshund.

The Monster By the Lake

By Rachel West

One average day, two sisters lived in a small home beside the lake (with their mother). Nearby was a dark forest (it was rather creepy, though). They have never been because they were forbidden from ever stepping a foot inside. People were worried about what vile creatures lurked deep inside. The reason was because three years ago monsters attacked which brought them fear of ever going back in. The oldest sister was named Abigail and the youngest was named Esme. They were both very adventurous and loved causing mayhem (because why not?) but would still behave when told to do so.

"C'mon Abigail, can't we just go in the sinister forest for five minutes, please?" pleaded Esme hoping for an answer which she knew she wouldn't get (sadly) but she would always try.

"No, of course not, you don't know what might be in there!" said Abigail with a tone of anger in her voice.

As the street began to darken the two girls were called in for tea like every usual day. While jogging along the small path Abigail heard a faint crash fade from the woods. "Wait, what was that sound?" muttered Abigail cautiously.

Esme replied, "Umm… I don't know, let's just get home, quick!" Back inside, they sat down on their little wooden chairs and began discussing what had just happened. "We must have just been hearing things" reassured Abigail.

Esme agreed and then stumbled off to bed with Abigail knowing that they were completely safe (or so they thought).

BANG!

"What was that?" cried Esme, absolutely terrified.

"I don't know! Should we go and have a look?" pondered Abigail, "Uh... let's just go!"

Silently, both the girls walked down the stairs while being very cautious about what was around them, but there was nothing. Extremely confused, they ran back into their rooms. Abigail was almost certain that something just wasn't right, but after a bit of thinking she went straight back to bed. Meanwhile, Esme was staring out into the woods with a look of confusion (pretty much the whole night).

That morning, when Abigail woke up from her half-peaceful sleep Esme had gone. Worrying a lot, she ran downstairs, hoping she was just watching TV, but was she? No, Abigail knew where she would be. Remembering the question Esme asked yesterday, it rang through her head every five seconds.

"I knew it!" thought Abigail, "Of course, she wanted to go in the woods, that's where she would be most suspicious of!"

Excitedly, Abi (her nickname) grabbed her brightest torch and ran. She felt the wind rush through her long brown hair, as she ran across the sunlit hills. Suddenly, all the nice bright feelings turned black: pitch black. Even though her stomach started turning with fear she was determined to find Esme. The trees started to cloud over her head and all of the grass went brown. The winding path suddenly faded as she began to create her own. Eventually she spotted Esme marvelling at a massive, abandoned house.

"ESME!" shouted Abi, delighted and furious at the same time, "What have you been doing?!"

"I-I-I-saw something inside, and it looked horrific," whimpered Esme, "I don't know what it is!"

"Are you sure it wasn't your imagination?" grumbled Abigail. After Esme had confirmed for sure she wasn't dreaming it, Abigail began to worry. If it was real, what could it be? Many questions clouded her mind in panic. "Right you'll probably never hear me say this again but we are going to go in, okay?" assured Abigail.

"Uhhhhh… ok, let's go in, I guess," replied Esme. Confidently, Esme lead the way through, making sure to step over the missing planks. The floor inside was cold and damp, but Abigail could see some mysterious foot prints going ahead (kind of). Both of them realising they could be in a very dangerous situation, but still walked on. An oddly shaped shadow just crossed a window, sending an eerie shiver down Esme's spine. "Umm… Abi did you see that?" asked Esme, in need for reassurance.

"Oh yeah… I-I did, oh no, ermm… lets go and take a look, but be very, and I mean very careful," answered Abigail confidently. Esme took a glance around the corner. She saw a huge, menacing, green coloured creature with blood red shot eyes. He was not what she expected to see as he was taller than their cottage. Abigail swiftly ran over. "W-W-W-What is that thing?!" shrieked Abigail anxiously, "Look at the size of those horns!"

"No wait, stop, please wait!" said the thing hopefully, "Will you help me? Please."

"Ok, with what?" questioned Abigail.

"Well, everyone thinks I'm some kind of monster, but I'm not, please make that clear to them," begged the beast.

93

"Of course we will, if you promise not to come in our house again," stated Esme.

The two girls said their goodbye and ran back out both agreeing that it was quite strange. When they got home they put up posters everywhere, which said that the beast was actually very friendly. They also occasionally would tell people they met not to worry about him. Therefore, any time someone sees him they do not run away in terror, but they say hello and are kind which ends up with him being kind back!

Beyond the Moon

By Harriet Grace Hockey

Brrrrrrrrrrrrrrrrrrrriiiiiiiiiiiiiiinnnnnnnnnnngggggggggggggg!

At 8 o clock in the morning, my alarm clock suddenly, but loudly, went off. I woke up and with a great big yawn; I bashed the alarm clock off. I tossed the covers down and got out of bed. I dressed in my favourite outfit, and then I walked to the window. It was a lovely sunny day. I did my hair, put my shoes on and went for a walk in the sun. I met a lovely girl, and she was very kind. I asked her name, and she said, "My name's Poppy!"

She asked me the same. I said, "My name's Izzabella!"

She also asked me, "What are you doing?" but before I could say anything, a mean boy came along, interrupted me, and said, "Read my lips - you don't deserve to be friends!"

Can you believe he said that to us? He was sooooooooooooooooooooooo mean! But then, some people around us copied him. People around the people around us copied. People around the people around the people around us copied. It took only seconds for the whole world to copy his unkindness, and everyone kept copying until the world was filled with meanness.

The world was filled with meanness, but at least me and Poppy were fine.

Poppy had a secret. It was the most precious to her. She had super powers! So, she flew to space with me. We saw the world was COVERED in grey and black because of all the meanness. Quickly, we hatched a plan to restore the beauty of the world.

One by one, we flew to each country and hypnotised everyone to give them back their souls full of kindness. Our plan was exhausting, but it was worth it! At the very last country, we tried to hypnotise the people, but somehow, it failed to work. It was the country that the mean boy was in. The mean boy and Poppy ended up in a BIG fight. Poppy used her teleportation power. She blasted the mean boy into another dimension! Poppy had won the fight!

At last, the final country turned back to normal. But, there was something on the ground. It was the mean boy's headphones! Poppy had an idea – she flew straight up to space with the headphones, and once she got there, she threw them high up into the air, and they disappeared beyond the moon!

Soon, the whole world couldn't help being kind. Poppy took me back into space to see the vibrant colours of the world restored. We were exploding with pride, and jumped up and down in a squeezy hug. What an amazing adventure. Who knew that my new friend had super powers!!! And of course, as Poppy and I knew all along...

KINDNESS RULES!!!

Amy Saves the World

By Beatrice Mae Hockey

Once upon a time there was a pretty princess called Lulu. She took care of the whole world. She loved everyone and she helped everyone.

There was a baddie called Maya. She thought the world was an idiot! She was a big bully in the whole wide world.

One day Maya pooped really really badness all over the planet. The whole planet was goopy and woopy brown and black. The whole planet was stinky winky. Everyone felt really sad.

"MWAHAHAHA," cackled Maya. "You look much prettier now you're covered in POO Princess Lulu!!!"

"You can't do this!" shouted Princess Lulu. She pulled out her superpowers to make a magical forcefield to stop the poop but it backfired and knocked her out!

Princess Lulu finally opened her eyes. All she could see was people being fighty and naughty. She was furious! She shouted at them but they kept fighting. So Princess Lulu called for Amy.

Amy was a big huge humungous saving super hero. She had short silver hair, a silver suit and galaxy boots up to her knees. Amy ran with super speed to Princess Lulu. When she saw Princess Lulu covered in poo she was furious!

"You are stinky! You need a shower!" she said. Amy shot laser beams from her eyes to Princess Lulu. She was soon back to normal. Then she looked at Maya. "Come here I've got something special to give you" Amy said.

"You can't stop me. I will make the whole wide world fight. Everyone will be under my control!" cried out Maya.

"Really? Try this" replied Amy. With a flash she banged Maya into a poopy bubble forcefield. The bubble floated into the sky. Amy zapped it with a galaxy strike and Maya went zooming to the moon.

"Ew! Poo!" shrieked Maya. At last she was gone.

Princess Lulu jumped and clapped in celebration. Then it was time to clean up the people and the world. They used their laser powers to clean everywhere up as fast as a lightning strike! soon the world was all sparkly again. Now the poop was gone everyone stopped being fighty and naughty. They hugged each other and said sorry. Maya hated her poopy bubble so much she decided to say sorry too.

The whole world was generous loving friends and they all lived happily ever after.

Easter Joy

By Keira Dinsley

I couldn't send a picture of my story so I thought I would email it to you. If you would please I'll tell you my story.

The random act of kindness is one that I have done not so long ago. Recently was the time that people on motorbikes would collect loads of Easter eggs from different stores and donate them to children's hospitals for the kids that don't have anyone to celebrate with, but due to the recent circumstances there was no one able to do this.

So a nice little group of people recently set up a charity where people could donate money and they would buy the eggs and get people with vans to pick them up and deliver them to the children's hospital. In response to this I gave 20 pounds of my birthday money to help. I was also able to persuade my family to also give some of their money in. In result I hope I helped out in some way and made some other kids happy.

P. S. Thank you if you read this, and I hope it is ok that there is more than 100 words I just didn't know how else to say it.

Thank you for your time.

Buddy's Story

By Millie Newton

One Saturday morning Samantha was getting ready for work. She worked in an animal shelter not to far from where she lived. She loved animals ever since she was little, and she always volunteered to help out with the animals. After Samantha had finished her education, she got a job with animals. When she was ready for work, she hopped in her car and drove off.

Halfway there her car suddenly stopped it then made weird noises, her first thought was the car had broken down and yes, she was right the car had broken down and she was not very happy about it. She called the AA and when they arrived, they confirmed she had accidentally run over something sharp on the road they fixed her car out and she got back in and carried on with her journey to work.

She looked at her watch and realised that she was half an hour late for work.

What was she going to tell her boss?

Her boss was like no other boss he was not supportive, he was nasty and cold hearted he only did the job for the money not because he enjoyed working and caring for animals.

Anyway, Samantha glanced out of the wing mirror and saw a strange figure lying on the side of the road she pulled over and got out of the car, she moved the bushes away and saw a dog! The first thing what came to her mind was the dog had been neglected and dumped, she couldn't just leave it lying there she had to take it to the vets, but she was already late for work.

Samantha was very worried that she would get fired for being late, just at that moment Samantha remembered that she had a spare lead in the boot of her car, she put the dog on the lead and put it in the car and drove to the closest vets. When she walked in there was only a lady with her cat, but the dog didn't seem to mind the cat, she sat for only a short while as the surgery wasn't that busy. When the vet called them in she lifted the dog on the table, the vet checked the dog and could tell that the dog had been neglected and starved, so they gave the dog some food and a bath, the dog was so hungry that it ate the food in 2 minutes flat, he was really hungry!

The vet said, "someone is going to have to take the dog and give it a permanent home".

Samantha replied, "I actually work in an animal shelter". After a thorough examination the vet told Samantha that the dog was male and around 2-3 years. Samantha drove to work and was pretty happy about what she had done today.

When she arrived at work her boss was standing at the door and he shouted, "SAMANTHA YOU ARE AN HOUR LATE!"

Samantha replied, "sorry boss I had to get my car fixed, it broke down on the motorway and I saw an abandoned dog on the side of the road, so I took him to the vets."

Samantha walked to the spare kennel unlocked it and put the dog inside. Samantha decided to name him Buddy. Buddy waited patiently for a few days for a family to adopt him, eventually a lady and her two kids came into the shelter, straight away the lady knew that her and her family wanted to adopt Buddy. The lady and her kids put Buddy in the car and drove away.

Samantha had a funny feeling that Buddy would not be happy with his new family. If only Samantha's parents would allow her to have a dog, she would have taken Buddy home with her. Her parents were very house proud, their house was spotless and they did not want dog hair on the carpets and any of the furniture chewed. Samantha tried to say not all dogs chew, but they didn't listen they were house proud she also told her parents how she rescued buddy and he needed a loving home.

One week later, the lady came back with the dog. Samantha was very confused.

The lady said "I would like to return this dog, it has chewed everything in the house."

She was furious, when she left Samantha felt really bad for Buddy, she managed to convince her parents to rehome Buddy with them, eventually they said yes, she was so happy. Later that day she took Buddy home, with lots of love, care and patience Buddy became a member of the family and Samantha was so happy.

Buddy and Samantha became the best of friends and were inseparable. This was the beginning of the adventures of Samantha and Buddy.

Jessie, the Little Brat

By Isabelle Brydon

My friend is turning into a monster!

Once upon time there was a girl called Sophie, she was very helpful and beautiful. She was the most popular person in school. Everybody was always crowding around her, she looked like she had a gazillion pounds! She had baby blue eyes, and bright blonde hair like Elsa, she always wore a bright, shining pink dress. She was as clever as Einstein and as caring as Mother Teresa.

Jessie, on the other hand, was beautiful but she always had a scowl on her face which made her look ugly. Her eyes were as green as grass and her hair was as red as fire, it was so wavy. She wore a bright yellow dress, it looked like shining stars falling from the sky.

Jessie and Sophie were best friends (but they were not alike). Sophie loved to be helpful but Jessie did not understand why Sophie should be helpful because Jessie thought it was a waste of time when you could be playing Roblox. Sophie was always trying to convince her. But Sophie kept on failing and Jessie just acted like a selfish little brat.

Early one Saturday morning, Sophie decided to call for Jessie so they could spend the day together. As they walked past Mrs Woods house they heard a loud noise, it sounded like she was falling over. Sophie ran to Mrs Wood's house and knocked on the door to see if she was fine, but Mrs Wood shouted "HELPPPPPPP!".

But the door was locked so Sophie said "I can't get in".

Sophie and Jessie went through the back door but Jessie rolled her eyes and said "come on let's go home, this is boring, I'm sure she's fine. I want to play Roblox!"

Sophie said "no, I am helping Mrs Wood, even if it takes 3 whole hours".

Jessie replied, "suit yourself then, I'm going home."

Sophie found Mrs Wood lying on the kitchen floor, Mrs Wood had stubbed her big toe, it was bleeding lots and she was in a lot of pain. Sophie helped Mrs Wood to a chair and called the doctor. While she was waiting she made her a cup of tea and chatted to her.

Mrs Wood said to Sophie "you're such a kind girl. What would I have done without you? I wish Jessie was like you."

When Jessie got home she started to play Roblox, she was playing Adopt Me because she wanted to go on her rideable Fennec Fox. She noticed that her arms were getting hairier, they were growing yellow fur!

Jessie said "omg, what is happening to me?". She ran downstairs and shouted "mum, mum. I'm turning into a monster!".

Her mum just looked at her and said "it's probably because you are not helping and are selfish."

Jessie said "I'm so sorry." (but she didn't mean it).

To try and stop herself from turning into a monster Jessie tried to help her mum, it did not work because she just wanted to play Roblox so kept complaining. As the days went on she became more and more mean so she kept on turning into a monster. After a week she was fully a monster. Her mum told her it would happen if she didn't change her selfish ways.

Meanwhile, Sophie missed her friend but she was as kind as ever and was forever known as the girl who did the most random acts of kindness in the town.

Always be kind or it might happen to you! No offence!

This is what Jessie looked like in the end...

A Random Act of Kindness

By Wendy Ransom

"Schools Out!" cried Josephine Goldman sprinting around and around the school yard. And it, indeed, was the last day of school. Josephine had been waiting for this day for weeks and weeks so she was very thrilled.

The irritated teachers,on the other hand, were clasping their hands over their ears and calling "Stop that this instant Miss Goldman, it's extremely annoying."

Josephine's classmates,unlike the teachers, cheered and laughed. Josephine was not silent but deadly, but loud and deadly. She was *REALLY* loud. She looked around, thinking herself as freestyle, kind and loving. She stopped dead when she looked at the playground corner. Timmy, the most unpopular kid in school, was huddled up there, sulking. She had to help. So she walked over and started to comfort him.

He still cries.

Then she got an idea. "Hey," she whispered in his ear. "You wanna be friends? I've got a spare cinema ticket, and if you want to be friends with me you can come with me."

Everyone in her school wanted to be friends with her. Everyone was shocked when Timmy came onto the playground holding Josephine's hand. This was definitely a random act of kindness. When she had woke up that morning she never expected to do this. All through lessons, lunch and break times people stared at her cheering up Timmy.

At break time she shouted some very rude words which she should not have even known (I will not mention any for yours and my sake). Timmy, by the end of the day, had a great big smile from ear to ear on his face.

"See you tomorrow?" asked Josephine hopefully. Timmy's eyes lit up even more than they already were.

"You mean it?!" he asked, eyes wide. " Yeah totally!" Josephine smiled her usual smile, but slightly bigger. She had never had a real friend before.

She sprinted all the way home until she got to her mum. "I've got... a friend... to take... to the... cinema," she panted, breathing.

Mum looked at her curiously "Who?" she asked.

Josephine had to catch her breath then replied: "Timmy Walker. He's my new friend. I helped him as my random act of kindness today." In the Goldman's house they had to do a random act of kindness each day. Josephine disliked this, but Mum had insisted.

For tea was Josephine's favourite, Macaroni cheese. "Mmmmm! Mac'n' cheese!" Josephine said as she sat down at the table. She had munched every golden mouthful by the time Dad got home from work as a doctor. For pudding was a rich creamy chocolate mousse, another one of Josephine's favourites. When she went to sleep in her bunk bed for bed time, it was 9pm. She swiftly climbed the ladder to the top bunk and tucked herself in as Mum turned off the light. She fell asleep nearly as soon as she tucked herself in.

She woke up early next morning so she fell back to sleep.

When she woke up next time it was 9am when she usually woke up. She rushed downstairs. After breakfast Timmy would arrive!

Mum came down not long after Josephine had come

down. She made breakfast and Josephine had nearly devoured it in 5 seconds. " Hey honeybun," said Mum soothingly. "Don't eat too fast! You'll be ill!"

"I'm excited that's all," said Josephine, still munching her toast. After breakfast, she sat on the windowsill, stiff. She was not aware of what was going on around her, like Mum packing for the cinema. She sat there until she heard the screech of wheels on the driveway. Timmy walked out, still smiling his big, happy smile. Josephine instantly unlocked the door and sprinted out, excitedly, to greet Timmy.

"So what are we watching?" asked Timmy, waddling inside the house.

"Terrifying Tuesday," said Josephine. "It's the sequel to Freaky Friday." She had watched Freaky Friday heaps of times, so it had begun to get a bit boring. She was quite excited about this next one, though. In the trailer it had a really cool bit which Josephine described as a big *BOOM!*

Timmy must have seen the trailer too, because his face lit up more than it had ever done because. " Oh yes, Josephine, yes!" He bounced up and down and skipped around the room.

Mum obviously saw disaster coming, but she was too late. Timmy knocked into a chest of drawers, knocking an insignificant glass cup to the ground.

"Phew," said Mum, getting the broom. She passed it to Dad, whom Josephine hadn't noticed. "Come on you two," said Mum, pointing towards the door. "We might be late, otherwise."

"Yay!" Timmy and Josephine shouted together, Josephine punching the air. She skipped into the car, dragging her coat along the ground. Timmy had to wear his coat, and put on some hand gel. He took longer to get into the car, because of this.

By the time they got to the cinema there was 5 minutes until the movie started. Everyone went for a quick wee, then they all sat down. This movie was in 3D, so they put on their thick, cardboard glasses. They watched the screen as it glowed, and started the movie. It was a very exciting story, with Jamie as the star. In the interval, the fun began. Josephine started a popcorn fight with Timmy, which resulted with the entire audience throwing ice cream, popcorn, fizzy pop and chocolate at each other. When they heard the movie again, they all hushed and watched in silence. Even the babies didn't cry. When the movie ended, everyone started the food fight again, except that everyone threw food boxes and packets because they had eaten the food.

It was the best fun Josephine had had in ages, Timmy in his life. He'd never had a real friend either. When they went home Timmy and Josephine got a delightful surprise. Timmy was staying for a sleepover! He was going to sleep on the bottom bunk of Josephine's bunk bed! She quickly rushed upstairs to show Timmy his bunk, where he should put his stuff and the most important one: where the toilet is!

The night was wonderful, Josephine and Timmy chatted all night and they even got a midnight snack! It was delicious too, with the leftovers of the chocolate mousse as pudding. Josephine now changed her mind. This was the best day (and night) of her life. It was so cool. The next day Timmy and Josephine played Granny! on Roblox. You had to run away from Granny, who couldn't go up the tree of the tree house. If she whacked you 3 times you lost, but you could play again. She usually stayed at the bottom, so Josephine mostly jumped down there. Timmy squealed when he first saw granny, while Mum freaked out, saying it would give them nightmares.

After that, Mum insisted they did aqua beads. So Josephine made an eagle, while Timmy made a smiley emoji. It was a while until they dried, so they played Mario kart on Josephine's Nintendo switch. She always won, even on the easy-peasy mushroom cup.

But the fun ended when they went back to school. There was a new kid, a bully, who always picked on Josephine and Timmy. He kicked and poked them in class. It happened like that until one day, Josephine got an idea. "We'll tell my admirers. They like me, so they'll fight for me!" She explained to Timmy, on Thursday. She knew she still had admirers, so their (her) plan would work easy-peasy simple-pimple, thought Josephine.

So the next day, she gathered her followers and explained: "David, the bully, is bullying me. Who will help me?" she said, hoping not to catch David's attention.

Nearly none of them put their hand up.

Josephine sighed, then said "I'll give you sweets if you help!"

All of them cheered and raised their hands, while Josephine chucked her sweets she had in her pocket (she knew this might happen, so she brought them) over the crowd.

They started munching, but once they were finished Josephine shouted "*CHARGE!*" in her loudest voice (which was extremely loud) and they all sprinted after her, shouting, screaming and shrieking. When they eventually found David they all ran towards him and fought with whatever they had, including mops, pans (these were the best) and chucking biscuits they had saved from lunch. Josephine stood in the middle of the battle, fighting David with one or two frying pans. In the end, David gave in, and swore to not bother Josephine or Timmy ever again.

Everyone cheered in delight, and chanted "Josephine, Josephine, Josephine!" She smiled proudly, now believing she was freestyle, kind and loving. She and Timmy were friends forever after that, seeing each other every single day, even when they were off. They were BFF's. Best Friends Forever. Josephine, for then on, did her random act of kindness every day merrily. It was wonderful to have a friend, she and Timmy knew that.

Will *you* do a random act of kindness today? I hope so!

The End

Gilesgate Story Challenge 2020

Top Bins Disaster!

———————————

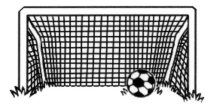

————————————

By Dylan and Chloe Skelton

Chloe was the teams top scorer, but as the season went on she started to miss more and more free kicks!

Chloe loved playing football and was the teams top scorer, but as the season flew by she noticed she started to miss more and more free kicks, curling the ball wide of the post more often than she scored. What was she going to do?

It was a hot summers day Chloe was playing football in the Gilesgate Cup Final, half an hour into the game, as she was about to shoot she was fouled, just on the edge of the D.

Chloe stepped up to take the free kick and

BANG!

...she curled the shot wide of the top corner!

She was very annoyed with herself. As half time struck the other teams goalkeeper came to talk to Chloe, she noticed he was wearing sports glasses.

"Why don't you go to Simon Berry's Opticians, he could help you with your eyesight like he helped me. It's just around the corner, you could be there and back before the second half starts."

Chloe set off for the opticians and it only took her a few minutes. When she arrived she saw lots and lots of glasses but the ones that stood out the most were the sparkly pink sports ones. Simon Berry welcomed her very kindly, after that he showed Chloe some capital letters on a chart.

Which were **NOPQXR** but Chloe said **AVWPRY.**

He also showed her a picture of a goal and asked "Can you see the Top Bins?"

"Noooooooo," said Chloe.

Simon replied, "try these" handing her the pink sparkly sports glasses.

Chloe said "I like them."

When she put them on she could see all the letters and The Top Bins.

She thanked Simon and ran off to play the second half.

Ten minutes in she was awarded another free kick.

She was very positive she was going to score.

She took a run up and

BANG!

...she found the top corner!

As the keeper picked the ball out of the back of the net Chloe ran over and thanked him for his help.

The End

My Book of Helpful Little Things

By Leola Christopher
at Durham Gilesgate Primary School

FRIENDS

I helped my very kind and caring friend to repay her for all of the nice things she has done for me. She had a cut in her foot so she had to hop. At break I offered to help her outside. She said yes so I half carried her, half dragged her out. She was sooo heavy! When we got onto the playground, the whistle blew so we had to go back in. It was very hard work!

PLAYING WITH MY BROTHER

I don't really like playing with my brother. I prefer sitting in my room reading a book and dreaming about being an author. So anyway, I went downstairs for something to eat and my brother was asking mam if she would play. She said "not now" so I reluctantly said I'll play. I can't eat a brother! I gave mam half an hour to relax. Good!

TIDYING

I stayed behind when the rest of my class went into singing assembly. I like singing but I wanted to tidy. I went around tidying away pencil cases. When I sorted out the pencil pots I found bogies, toe nails, blood, spit and even eye balls! I am never staying behind again!

WASHING

When I was taking dirty clothes out of the washing basket, I saw a squid! I screamed but then I realized that it was just a shirt. The next day I dried the washing. I saw the squid again but this time it was real! I opened the window and chucked it out. Phew, that was close!

The Magic Pencil

By Mya Pallister

One day a little girl called Ruby was strolling around the streets with her dog but suddenly she heard a loud THUMP! She looked down and saw an odd pencil on the hard concrete path. She was walking back home when she saw a little sparkle come from the top of the pencil. So instead of walking back home, she went to help people out.

While she was walking down town, Ruby saw a homeless man and decided to give him some thing but she didn't know what to give him. Then she saw an old lady who was struggling to walk on her own, so she wanted to help out the old lady. While she was walking , Ruby saw her best friend called Mia and saw her fall over! So then Ruby asked her, "are you ok?"

Mia cried, "No my knee is bleeding!".

All of a sudden, she dropped the pencil and it rolled and rolled until it stopped, then she picked it up and saw the writing on the pencil that said '1 draw per each person.' She finished reading and thought, "I wonder what I should do?"

So then she thought of an idea which was to give some thing they would really need in life. She went to the homeless man and said, "I have a surprise for you," and she drew a house for the homeless man.

He said, "thank you very much now I don't need to worry".

Then Ruby went to the old lady and said, "I see you need some help so let me help you," then Ruby drew a mobility scooter so she could get around faster.

Then Ruby went to her friend and said, "here have this for your knee," and she drew Mia a plaster with the pencil.

Mia replied, "thank you so much, have a good day!"

We should all care for one another and the world will be a better place.

For Those Who Need it Most

By Jasmin Henderson-Gray

It was a beautiful summer day. Flowers were blooming, the trees were swaying and you could hear the trickling of the stream. The sky was graciously clear and the sun was mercilessly beaming down on everyone. The street was full of people enjoying the sun: there were children and dogs playing and people relaxing in their gardens. I have just moved here and everyone seems so nice so I just felt like I had to do something nice for them, even if it was just something small.

Later in the afternoon the heat had risen and everyone was sweltering in the sun. As I walked out of my house I saw an old homeless man sitting on the pavement. He looked weak and extremely warm, so I got in my car and drove to the nearest shop to buy some water and food for him. When I came back he was still there and looked even more dehydrated than before. When I brought the water to him he turned it away but he needed something to drink so I left it on the pavement for him to see if he would take it.

Furthermore, I still felt bad for him so I made him some food and went back to see if he was still there. I noticed that the water was gone. I wondered if someone had taken it so I went and got him a new one and brought it out to him with the food. He wasn't eating or drinking any of the stuff I brought out for him and I was getting really worried. When I went to bed that night all I could think about was him and how lonely he must be.

When I woke up in the morning he was gone and the plate and an empty bottle there. All I could hope was that he was safe.

Retyred

By Catherine Potter

While being in lockdown with a lot of free time on my hands I decided that I was going to help out all the old residents of my area by giving them a free gift.

I have been using my old tyres to make swan planters and then I painted them adding a flower to the centre. This looks really nice and will keep a nice smile on their face during these terrible times we are facing at the moment due to coronavirus. I am going to deliver them in one of my daily 1h exercises.

I hope to put a smile on their face and keep them happy in these bad times.

I also painted a tyre swan in the colours green yellow and white for the north air ambulance and walked a few doors from my house, knocked on the door, put the swan down and moved away from the door. When he saw it he was the most happy and said it was an excellent idea and well done.

I was so happy I put joy into someone's life.

About the Team

Simon Berry

Simon has been an Optometrist for over 20 years. He opened his own community Optometry Practice in 2002.

He gets bored quickly and has lots of little projects to keep life more interesting. One of the ones he is most proud of is the Gilesgate Story Challenge.

He is passionate about books and when flirting with a different career he did try and write a few himself. (None were ever published.) He had a literary agent for a while but they left soon after to become a coffee barista and he lost his contract. He hopes this wasn't because of having him as a client.

Contact Simon at:
simon@simonberry.co.uk

Or visit the Practice website:
www.simonberry.co.uk

Vicki Sparks

I absolutely love a good story! In my job as a football commentator and reporter, story-telling is everything, as we draw on the power of words to paint pictures and inspire emotion.

It's a joy and a privilege to be able to do this - and it's been a joy and a privilege to see such imagination and creativity running through the entries for this year's Gilesgate Story Challenge!

Thank you to each and every single one of you who has contributed to this book: keep writing, keep speaking, and keep telling each other stories!

Tim Cole

Tim is a part time illustrator / full time eye guy. He met Simon through the eye world having helped him with his eye scanning machine.

By day Tim usually can be found driving around hospitals trying to get eye departments to buy eye scanners and on evenings and weekends he tries to keep his toes in his arty routes with caricatures and drawings.

Miles Nelson

Miles is an author from Durham. Whilst he loves to tell stories of his own, his favourite thing in the world is to help and inspire young writers to hone their skills.

Miles specializes in sci-fi and fantasy, although he has a special soft spot for nature writing. His first book, entitled *Riftmaster*, is due to be released in 2021.

An interesting fact about Miles is that he enjoys collecting books about animals, from the fantastical to those we see every day.

Contact Miles:

milesnelson1997@outlook.com

milesnelsonofficial.wordpress.com

@Probablymiles

Esther Robson

I've always loved to read so was delighted to be invited to join the Gilesgate Story Challenge 2020 team, it has been such a pleasure and great fun to work with Simon, Tim, Miles and Vicki.

I've been genuinely amazed at the standard of the entries and the talent and imagination these young writers have. I have been transported to Florida and walked with dragons and unicorns and it was so heartwarming to read the wonderful acts of kindness – especially this year. It has been a truly uplifting experience.

About our Cause

Each year, the money raised from the Gilesgate Story Challenge is put towards a fantastic cause, and this year's competition is no different. To fit with this year's theme of kindness and love, this year's two charities are focused on mental health, giving people who are struggling a place to go and someone to talk to.

RTProjects is an independent registered charity. Our aim is suicide prevention.

We provide art therapy sessions for people suffering from depression or anxiety related disorders.

We provide a safe, nurturing environment free from stigma where people can take the time they need to recover.

Over the course of lockdown, we have seen many acts of kindness from volunteers and clients.

One of our volunteers heard that one of our pals had broken his ankle during lockdown. Realising the isolation he could be facing she managed to locate a wheelchair and took him out in it once a week.

Instead of cancelling our milk delivery at RTProjects Alice has been delivering it to pals who can't leave the house. This means so much more than the bottle of milk. It's a genuine connection with the outside word. It also keeps our milkman in employment.

RTProjects has set up a private 'Whats app' group for pals to connect and share their artwork. This has been a life saver for this who are alone and facing the challenge of isolation.

The Cheesy Waffles Project is a registered charity for children, young people, and adults with additional needs. Although our project is predominantly for people with learning disabilities it is not exclusive to and everyone is welcome to attend.

We rely on funding from grants, donations and fundraising to subsidise our activities to ensure they are affordable and inclusive for all.

The project continues to grow and works within the local community to support cohesion and to raise disability awareness through positive events and programmes.

Project members can gain a variety of Awards and Accreditation delivered by our qualified staff team including ASDAN Short Courses, Arts Award, The Duke of Edinburgh's Award, V Involved Award, and in-house awards.

Members have the opportunity to take part in residentials, trips away, shopping excursions, meals out, sports activities, cookery programmes etc. This gives them an opportunity to go out without support from their family giving respite to carers but also developing independent skills.

We encourage engagement in community work making gifts for others, working with local trusts, fundraising for chosen charities and supporting local community projects this raises self-esteem and confidence and raises the profile of the disabled people in their community.

All project members learn skills through taking part in activities that will help them with the transition into a happy and healthy adulthood and promote self-awareness and independency.

Most importantly we believe that every person no matter what their disability, background or beliefs deserve to have the same opportunities in life to help promote the learning of new skills, try new activities, visit new places and most importantly have fun.

The End

Thank you so much, from all of us, for joining us for this
year's Gilesgate Story Challenge. We hope you enjoyed
the stories, and we'll see you again next year!